First published in German as *Ein Geschenk vom Nikolaus* by NordSüd Verlag, Zürich. This English edition published in 2018 by Floris Books, Edinburgh. © 1994 NordSüd Verlag AG. English text © 2018 Floris Books. All rights reserved. No part of this book may be reproduced without the prior permission of Floris Books, Edinburgh. www.florisbooks.co.uk British Library CIP Data available. ISBN 978-178250-543-3 Printed in Malaysia

Santa Claus
and the
Christmas Surprise

Dorothea Lachner & Maja Dusíková

Floris
Books

Once, there was a sleepy village where it had snowed
all day and all night. Before long, all of the houses were
covered in a thick blanket of white.

The grocer couldn't open his shop. The baker couldn't sell her bread. Old Mr Gregory couldn't get to the barn to feed his goats. And there weren't any letters for the postman to deliver.

It was Christmas Eve, and in every home children were waiting, hoping that Santa Claus would come.

Anna and Michael were blowing little circles on their frosty window and peering outside.

"Santa Claus definitely won't be able to reach us this year," said Michael, sighing.

"He will!" said Anna.

"He won't!" grumbled Michael.

"You'll see," replied Anna. "He'll pull on his mittens, put on his scarf and strap on his skis. Santa always comes on Christmas Eve."

"But how will he get through the snow?" asked Michael.

"He will find a way and we'll have a happy Christmas. If we wish as hard as we can, Santa will hear us."

Anna and Michael wished as hard as they could, and their wish flew out of the village, past barns, over fields and through the forest. After a very long journey, it landed in Santa's beard. From there, it didn't take long to reach his ear.

"Ah," murmured Santa, listening very carefully to the wish. "Well, I'll see what I can do."

Santa thought very hard about what gifts he should bring to make sure everyone in the village had a happy Christmas.

"I don't think sweet treats are quite right this time," he muttered. "I don't think toys will do the job either."

Suddenly, he remembered something. "That's it!" he cried, climbing up to a high shelf. "The perfect surprise gift!"

With lots of rustling and crinkling of paper, Santa carefully wrapped the gift and packed it in his sack.

He pulled on his mittens, put on his scarf, strapped on his skis and set off into the dark night.

Santa whizzed through the forest, over fields
and past barns until he reached the village.
Deep snow lay all around and icicles hung from
every roof. Everyone was indoors and the air
was still and quiet.

From their cosy beds, Anna and Michael heard a faint whoosh of skis and the sound of boots trudging through the thick snow.

They looked at each other, jumped up and ran to the window. There, in the middle of the village, stood a large, mysterious sack.

"Santa's been!" whispered Michael. "Can we go and see?"

"It's not Christmas yet," said Anna. "We'll have to go back to bed and wait until morning."

As the sun rose on Christmas morning, the neighbours
noticed the sack too.

"What could it be?" they wondered.

"Is it from Santa?"

"Who is it for?"

Everyone wanted to open the sack, but the deep snow was blocking their way.

So the villagers fetched their snow shovels and began to dig. The children helped too, and slowly they cleared the paths until the villagers could finally reach the sack.

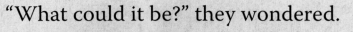

They stood around it, feeling warm and cheerful
after all their digging, wondering what could be inside.
"I think it's an oven!" said the baker.
"Or a barrel of apple juice," guessed the grocer.

"Or a bale of hay for my hungry goats?" suggested old Mr Gregory.

"Perhaps it's enough cough medicine to last all winter!" called the doctor, and everyone laughed.

"I hope it's a giant teddy bear!" shouted one of the children.

"Let's unwrap it!" cried Michael.

In the sack, they found a box. It was beautifully wrapped and tied with a bow. Excited, they started to unwrap it.

Inside the box was a slightly smaller box. Inside that was another, then another…

As they took turns to peel off layers, the gift grew smaller and smaller, and the mountain of paper and boxes grew bigger and bigger.

Finally, there was only one very small package left to open.

Anna, Michael and the other children unwrapped the final layer, as the villagers watched.

"A TEAPOT?" they all chorused in surprise.

"What kind of Christmas gift is that?" someone grumbled.

"We can't play with it," whined a child.

"But a hot drink *would* warm us up," said the baker.

"Now we've cleared the snow, let's all go back to my house for a cup of tea," said old Mr Gregory. "It's warm and cosy in my living room."

The teapot made enough tea for everyone. The baker
shared out bread and biscuits. Anna and Michael fetched
a basket of nuts.

"Happy Christmas everyone!" Old Mr Gregory raised his cup.
"It's been a pleasure spending Christmas with you all."

The villagers ate and drank and laughed and played, and
spent a wonderful day together.

Michael smiled. "Santa did reach us after all, didn't he?"

"He brought everyone a happy Christmas," agreed Anna. "We should say thank you."

So they both wished as hard as they could, and their thank you flew out of the village, past barns, over fields and through the forest until it reached Santa's ear.

"You're very welcome," said Santa, far away. "Happy Christmas everyone!"